A PROMISE TO GROW

A PROMISE TO GROW

COMMUNITY GARDEN

Marc Boston
illustrated by Ariel Mendez

Dedications

A very special thank you goes to the following creatives for coming together to bring this project to life:

Editors – Wednesday Edits
Illustrator – Ariel Mendez
Book Designer – mitchell&sennaar communications, inc.

We'd like to recognize and extend our heartfelt gratitude to the individuals and organizations who provided their invaluable contributions toward making this project a reality:

City of Promise
Peyton Lewis
The Virginia Humanities
The W. K. Kellogg Foundation
Jefferson School African American Heritage Center
Pam Evans
C. Jumoke Boston
Andrea Boston

"A Promise To Grow" © 2021 Marc Boston

ISBN-13: 978-0-9986899-0-6

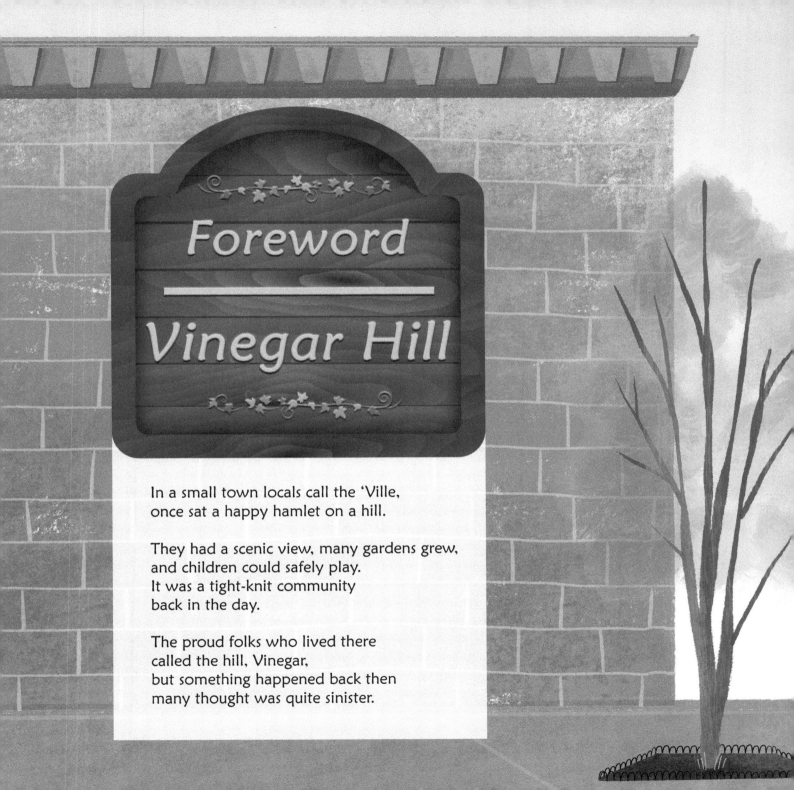

Foreword

Vinegar Hill

In a small town locals call the 'Ville,
once sat a happy hamlet on a hill.

They had a scenic view, many gardens grew,
and children could safely play.
It was a tight-knit community
back in the day.

The proud folks who lived there
called the hill, Vinegar,
but something happened back then
many thought was quite sinister.

While the residents focused on
building strong family ties,
they were being watched
by envious eyes.

The powers that be were hatching a plot
to take this land without a second thought.

Property developers liked what they saw,
so they seized the land using an unjust law.

They coveted the area, there was no debate,
since Vinegar Hill sat on prime real estate!

A scheme was hatched to block their vote,
and this land was lost as history will note.

Developers were allowed to act with impunity,
to snatch and shatter a thriving community.

Once they gained the upper hand,
they slowly began to sell off the land.

"Urban Renewal" was the stated intent,
and the people were forced
from their own settlement.

This section of town,
which was once renowned,
saw bulldozers roll in
to tear it all down.

This vibrant community was ripped apart,
injustice was the reason friends had to part.

Shopkeepers, teachers, barbers, and cooks
had their livelihoods snatched by laws
on the books.

1965

VINEGAR HILL
THE HEART OF
CHARLOTTESVILLE
BLACK BUSINESS
DISTRICT

CHARLOTTESVILLE

Restaurants, markets,
churches and shops...
demolished from the foundations
to the rooftops.

Daughters, sons, fathers, and mothers
all wondered if they would ever recover.

They searched for new homes,
which were hard to find,
because of bigoted rules
and how the system was designed.

There was one section of town
they were directed to go,
and what would become of them there,
they did not know.

Led to believe an honest deal
had been made,
but swapping a house for a unit
isn't a fair trade.

The people were left
without much to show,
but that's how it was
under old Jim Crow!

It wasn't their beloved Vinegar,
but they'd have to make do.
The people had hope
that they could begin anew.

And so began the dawn of a new age –
the founding of a community, Westhaven,
within 10th and Page.

VINEGA
1965
VINEGAR HILL
THE HEART OF
CHARLOTTESVILLE'S
BLACK BUSINESS
DISTRICT
NEIGH

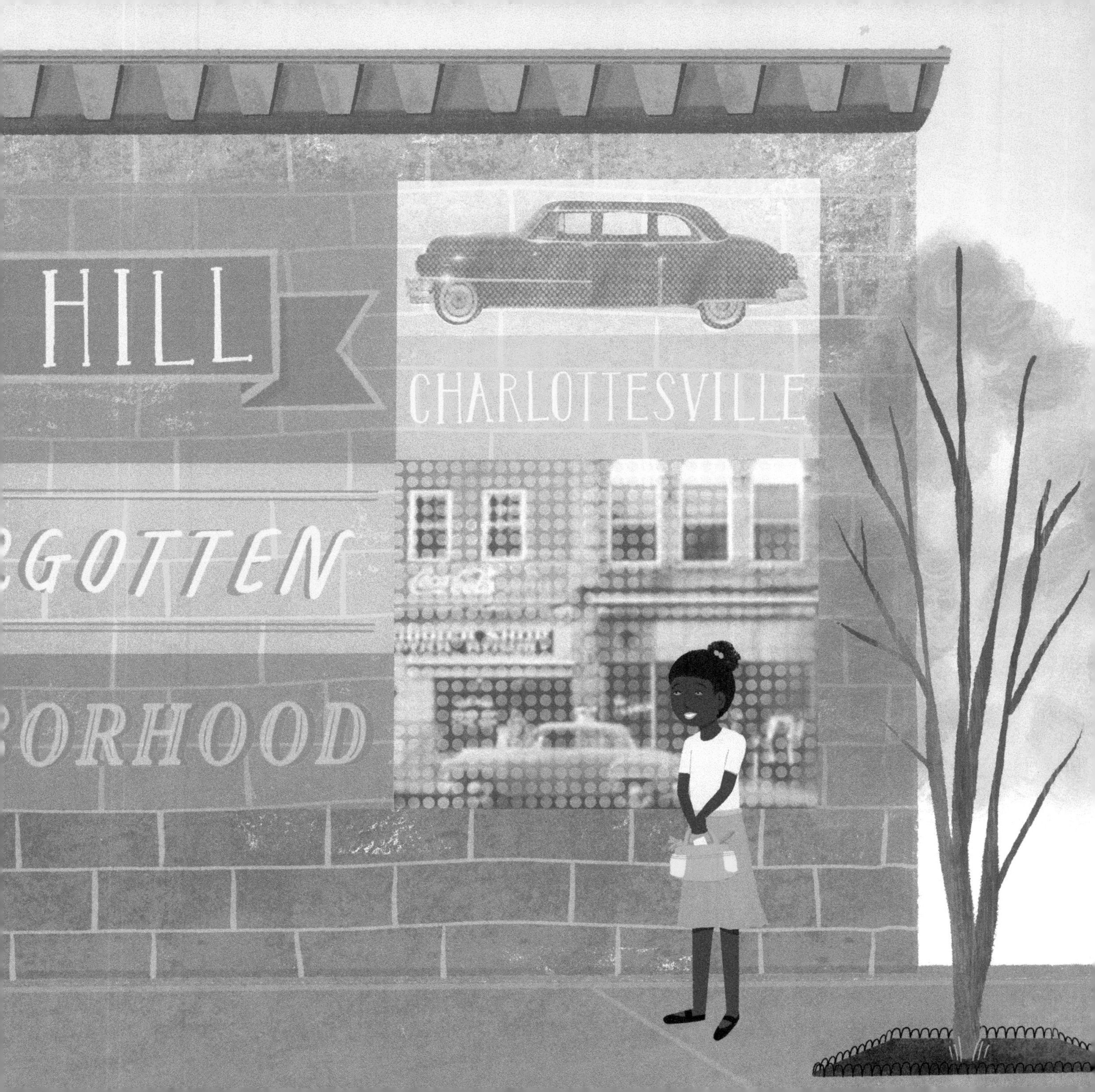
HILL
CHARLOTTESVILLE
GOTTEN
ORHOOD

Westhaven
A boy named CJ

There once was a boy who lived in Westhaven,
who was a kind and intelligent, young sports maven.

He loved baseball, wrestling, and video games,
and around the neighborhood he was highly-acclaimed

for being a do-gooder, who seemed to understand
that it was always better to lend a helping hand.

If there was a kid you could count on for support,
it was Charles Nathaniel Jackson, *CJ* for short.

CJ sought to be of service more often than not.
He was great to have around, a real *Johnny-on-the-spot!*

He dreamt of becoming a doctor

or studying the law.

Or maybe an illustrator because he loved to draw.

He was a thoughtful kid,
not into fashion or bling,
and creating with his hands
was his favorite thing.

Around 4 o'clock
he visited Ms. Mary Thomas
who ran an afterschool program
called *City of Promise*.

City of Promise

City of Promise is where the kids go
to have a lively place to learn and grow.

It was a wonderful gem and really quite rare,
filled with fun activities and people who care.

There was hiking,

cooking, and music too!

At *City of Promise*,
there was always something to do.

CJ used his time wisely, and began to thrive.
And while tending the garden, CJ came alive.

It was once overgrown with weeds, an old forgotten space.
But this was a project he was quick to embrace!

He read about planting
in a gardening book he'd found,
and just couldn't wait to plant
veggie seeds in the ground.

But before he could dream
of planting the seeds,
he must first proceed
to remove all the weeds.

Then came the part he loved the most –
spreading the fertilizer and the compost.

With a little water and tender loving care,
CJ's garden was just about there.

Before long, the plants had grown to their prime,
and CJ realized it was vegetable harvest time!

By listening to the beat of his own drum,
CJ learned that he had quite a green thumb.

Ms. Keys

One of CJ's favorite neighbors was Ms. Keys.
She was a nice older lady he loved to appease.

He and his friends sometimes formed a group,
and visited Ms. Keys while she sat on her stoop.

They'd gather around while she regaled them with stories
covering many topics, issues, and categories.

She lived an interesting life, this set her apart,
and her home was filled with tapestries and African art.

She'd tell them, *"It's important to learn your history,
this is the only way to erase the mystery."*

But as she got older and began to slow down
she was finding it harder to get around town.

It was becoming such a burden, such a great chore
to conjure enough energy to get to the store.

As it turned out, it had been quite a spell
since Ms. Keys was able to really eat well.

A great idea popped into CJ's mind
to do something charitable, compassionate, and kind.

He gathered the tomatoes, broccoli, and peas,
and personally delivered a batch to Ms. Keys.

Such a lovely gesture, it was wonderful indeed,
but Ms. Keys wasn't the only neighbor in need.

It was certainly a travesty, and there was no excuse
that the neighborhood had no easy access to fresh produce.

Inspired by what he'd learned, CJ rounded up recruits
and went door-to-door delivering his vegetables and fruits.

So pleased with what CJ was able to provide,
the whole neighborhood was happy and satisfied.

However, CJ wasn't about to stop there.
He was planning something remarkable – beyond compare.

It would be an endeavor that was fun, community-oriented, charitable, altruistic, and unprecedented!

He envisioned a tremendous opportunity
for a larger garden to support the whole community.

This venture was urgent, it simply could not wait.
Westhaven needed to grow its own food – it was time to cultivate!

The Westhaven Garden

They found a huge lot. It would be a rough start.
Everyone was going to have to do their part.

Their garden began to flourish to everyone's delight,
thanks to CJ exhibiting his valuable insight.

Imagine the joy felt as a result of all their toil,
when they reaped their delicious bounty from beneath the soil.

The community came together to manifest something great.
Now every household had fruits and veggies on their plate.

CJ was honored as the man-of-the-hour
by showing skill, courage, and willpower.

It often takes just one person with a vision to show
what a community can achieve, when they come together to grow.

VINEGAR HILL

Afterword
By Dr. Andrea Douglas & Jordy Yager

On November 1, 1870, a man named John West bought a piece of land in the center of Charlottesville for $100 in an area that would soon became known as the Vinegar Hill neighborhood. Mr. West was just 20 years old at the time, and had been held captive in a system of slavery that was abolished just five years earlier. This was also true for 53% of the area's Black population.

Vinegar Hill was one of Charlottesville's largest African American communities, and one of the oldest continuous neighborhoods in all of Charlottesville, Black and white. For nearly a century, Vinegar Hill remained a thriving community until *Urban Renewal*** forced people to move. In 1964, some moved 1/2-mile west, becoming the first residents of the newly constructed Westhaven neighborhood, which was named for John West. They took with them the knowledge of the historic importance of Vinegar Hill.

Mr. West himself lived and raised his children on West Main Street, in the heart of Vinegar Hill's business district. Mr. West was a barber by profession, but by the time of his death in 1927, he was considered a wealthy man who had bought and sold hundreds of properties to Black families all throughout the city and surrounding counties.

There are different interpretations of Vinegar Hill's exact geographic boundaries, however the neighborhood was generally considered to stretch from West Main Street (south) to Preston Avenue (north), and from 4th Street NW (west) to Preston Ave (east). Many who lived in the community made it possible for their neighbors to start their businesses and to buy homes.

Although restricted by Jim Crow segregation laws, a group of Black residents formed the Piedmont Industrial Land Improvement Company, and together bought dozens of properties across Charlottesville—from Fifeville to Rose Hill—stationing their headquarters at the top of Vinegar Hill, near the intersection of West Main Street and 4th Street NW.

AFTERWORD *(continued)*

Vinegar Hill also served as the community's educational core, and the center of religious and social life. In 1895, the Jefferson Graded School was established there, and later, in 1926, was expanded to become the only high school for Black students in the city. In addition to fraternal organizations and benevolent societies, such as the Freemasons, the Elks, the Order of the Eastern Star, and Odd Fellows, there were six Black churches within a 1/4-mile of each other: First Baptist, Mt. Zion, Zion Union Baptist, Ebenezer Baptist, Trinity Episcopal, Shiloh Baptist, and for a short period, a Methodist church.

For decades Black businesses thrived on Vinegar Hill: doctors and dentists, barbers and tailors, restaurants and grocery stores, taxi companies and pool halls, newspapers and funeral homes. One of the longest functioning businesses was Inge's Grocery Store. Opened in 1891 when George P. Inge bought the land on the northeast corner of West Main Street and 4th Street NW for $3,000, it served the community until ultimately closing in 1978.

In many ways this history of Vinegar Hill is the history and legacy of Westhaven.

** Urban Renewal was a federal program in which municipalities across America destroyed hundreds of thousands of homes it deemed unfit, with the oft-unkept promise of reinvesting taxpayer dollars into the area. In Charlottesville, homes in the Vinegar Hill, Garrett Street and Cox's Row neighborhoods were torn down under Urban Renewal, forcing many businesses to permanently close. In Vinegar Hill, 507 residents were forced to find new homes, according to the Charlottesville Redevelopment Housing Authority—463 of those were African American, and 44 were white.

Word Glossary & Phrases

Impunity – to be free from punishment; to do whatever you want to get your way.

Maven – an expert, a pro at something.

Appease – to make someone comfortable and satisfied.

Stoop – a staircase leading into a home.

Regaled – to entertain by telling a great story.

Conjure – to magically make something happen or appear.

Travesty – something that's so terrible that it seems like a joke.

Altruistic – to care about the wellbeing of others.

Unprecedented – unlike anything experienced before.

Flourish – to grow very well.

Toil – to work very hard.

Reaped – to collect or gather up.

Bounty – a prize or reward.

"Johnny-on-the-spot" – a person who is ready to help when needed.

"Green Thumb" – to be talented at growing plants.

"The powers that be" – individuals or groups in authority.

City of Promise

Proceeds from this book benefit *City of Promise*, a nonprofit organization committed to a family literacy approach of educational support in Charlottesville, Virginia.

If you would like to further support *City of Promise*, please visit http://www.cityofpromise.org to make a direct donation.

ABOUT THE AUTHOR

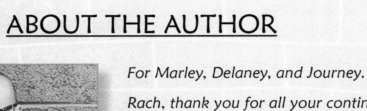

For Marley, Delaney, and Journey.

Rach, thank you for all your continued support.
Thanks Ma, for always knowing.

Marc Boston is a father, husband and children's book author. He has three daughters and a beautiful wife who inspire him every day. His mission is to create stories that emphasize the importance of diversity and inclusion and reflect on topics surrounding definitions of family values and self-empowerment. He has written and published three children's books: *"The Girl Who Carried Too Much Stuff," "What About Me"* and *"Dad Is Acting Strange."* All are available at www.marcboston.com. You can follow his journey on www.facebook.com/marcgboston and www.instagram.com/marcgboston/

ABOUT THE ILLUSTRATOR

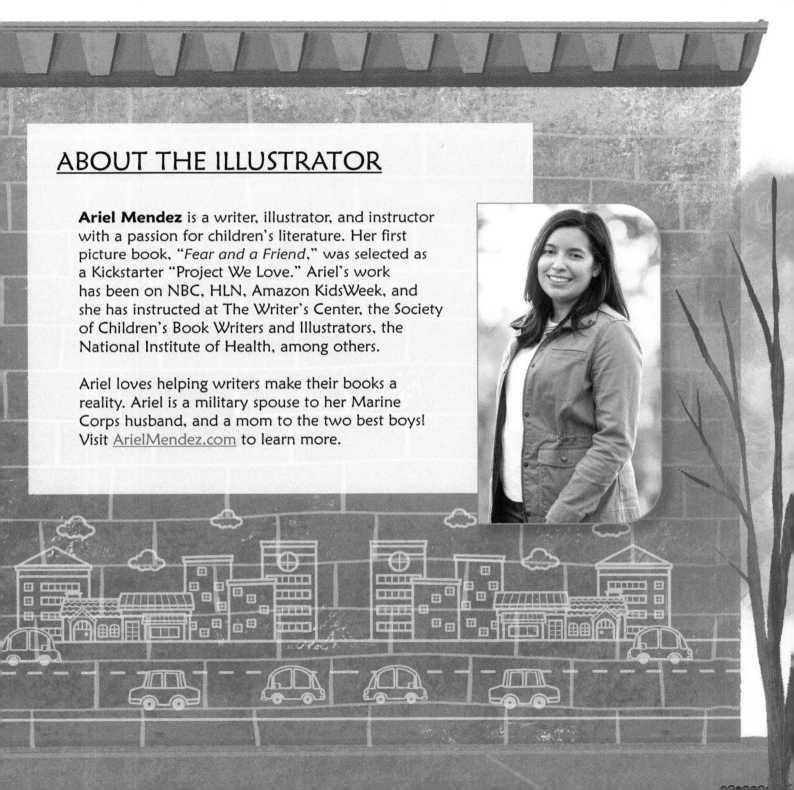

Ariel Mendez is a writer, illustrator, and instructor with a passion for children's literature. Her first picture book, "*Fear and a Friend*," was selected as a Kickstarter "Project We Love." Ariel's work has been on NBC, HLN, Amazon KidsWeek, and she has instructed at The Writer's Center, the Society of Children's Book Writers and Illustrators, the National Institute of Health, among others.

Ariel loves helping writers make their books a reality. Ariel is a military spouse to her Marine Corps husband, and a mom to the two best boys! Visit ArielMendez.com to learn more.